Everyone Belongs

United States Conference of Catholic Bishops

In Partnership with Loyola Press

Illustrated by Kristin Sorra

LOYOLA PRESS.
A JESUIT MINISTRY

UNITED STATES CONFERENCE OF CATHOLIC BISHOPS

LOYOLA PRESS.
A JESUIT MINISTRY

3441 N. Ashland Avenue
Chicago, Illinois 60657
(800) 621-1008
www.loyolapress.com

Author: United States Conference of Catholic Bishops
Department of Justice, Peace and Human Development/
Ad hoc Committee Against Racism

Contributing Editor: Susan Blackaby
Cover design: Loyola Press
Illustrations: Kristin Sorra

ISBN: 978-0-8294-4892-4

Library of Congress Control Number: 2019951063
Printed in the United States of America.
19 20 21 22 23 24 25 26 27 28 Bang 10 9 8 7 6 5 4 3 2 1

Loving Father,

Thank you for creating

all the children of the world, who

    live in many lands,

    have many traditions, and

    speak many languages.

Help me know that

you made each of your children unique

and you love each of them.

Help me be a friend

to children who are different from me,

for we are all part of your family!

Amen.

"Good game. Good game. Good game." Sam Kelly followed his best friend, Ray Ikanga, through the high-five line, congratulating the winning team.

Sam's older brother, Carter, was one of their coaches. He met the team by the bench. "You guys had a strong first half," he said, "but here's the deal. You can't let the other team get ahead. When you do, they win." With that, the boys got ready to leave.

Sam, Carter, and Ray were still talking about the game when Ray's mom drove up.

"Sam, don't forget you are coming home with me," said Ray. "I've got a surprise!"

Sam stuffed his sweatshirt into Carter's duffel bag. "Can you take this home for me? See you later," he said.

As Mrs. Ikanga drove through the neighborhood, Sam tried to guess what Ray's surprise was.

"Is it bigger than a shoebox?" asked Sam.

"Much, much bigger," said Ray.

"Is it alive?"

"Oh yes!" Ray laughed. "It is full of life!"

"A dog!" Sam said. "Did you get a dog?"

"No way," said Mrs. Ikanga.

Sam guessed and guessed, but he didn't even come close.

"Getting colder," said Ray. "You are so cold, Sam, that you're almost in the refrigerator."

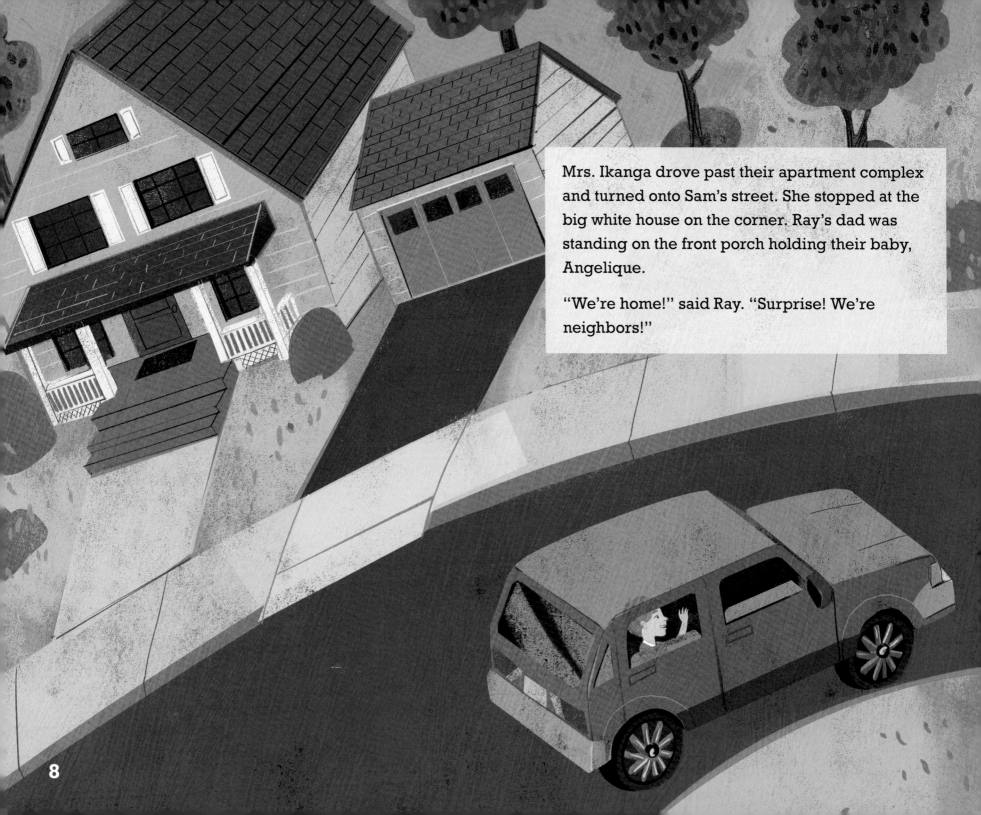

Mrs. Ikanga drove past their apartment complex and turned onto Sam's street. She stopped at the big white house on the corner. Ray's dad was standing on the front porch holding their baby, Angelique.

"We're home!" said Ray. "Surprise! We're neighbors!"

Sam couldn't believe it. He'd seen a moving van at the end of his street that morning and had hoped someone nice with kids would move in.

"This is even better than a dog," he said, hopping out of the car.

"Almost," said Ray.

"Are you kidding me?" Sam laughed. "This is perfect!"

"Even more perfect when we paint it yellow," Mrs. Ikanga said. "Like the sun."

It didn't take long for the families to become good neighbors and even better friends. The families shared rides and recipes. Sam's dad gave Ray's dad a rake as a housewarming present. Sam thought that having Ray in the neighborhood was the best, and for a few weeks, everything was fine.

Then, one evening after soccer practice, Mrs. Ikanga pulled into their driveway with Sam and Ray in the back seat. The headlights lit up the garage door like a movie screen. Someone had used red spray paint to leave a message in giant letters.

Ray leaned forward and told his mom not to stop. *"Vite, Maman!"* he said.

Mrs. Ikanga's hands were shaking as she reversed out of the driveway and pulled over to call Dr. Ikanga. Dr. Ikanga called Sam's parents, and Sam's mom came out to meet them at the curb. Mrs. Ikanga and Sam's mom embraced, then helped everyone get inside Sam's house. Before long, Dr. Ikanga arrived and joined them.

The boys waited in Sam's room while Dr. Ikanga and Sam's dad talked with the police. Sam could hear their moms speaking in the living room. They felt confused and scared. "Who would do something like that?" Sam asked, but Ray didn't answer.

Ray stood up, his fists clenched. "It said *go home.*" Ray had a steely look in his eyes, and he sounded angry. "Where is home? We lived in the campus apartments while my dad was in school. We lived in the big green hotel in Boston."

Hearing Ray's voice, Dr. Ikanga came upstairs. He said, "You're too young to remember, Ray, but before we came to the United States, we lived in a refugee camp in Uganda during the war. And before that, I lived in a northern Congolese village, where I met your mother. It was hard to leave and hard to come to a new land, but I know this: home is where we make it."

Ray nodded. "Every place has been home. My home is always with me."

Smiling, Dr. Ikanga said, "You sound much like a turtle. The shell is its home, which it carries wherever it goes."

Dr. Ikanga said that the police would increase patrolling in the neighborhood. "Let's go home," he said.

Ray turned to Sam. "See you later," Ray said. Sam hoped this was true.

WE ARE MADE IN GOD'S IMAGE

Ray didn't come to school the next day. Everyone had seen the news reports about the neighborhood hate crime, and Sam's classmates were talking about the interview with Dr. Ikanga while they waited for their social studies class to begin. Sister Bridget started the lesson.

"In just a few hundred years, the United States has become home to people from every part of the world," she said. "Some came willingly. Others were enslaved, bought and sold as property. In our last lesson, we learned that native peoples had been in the U.S. long before any new arrivals. The Native American people, who consisted of many diverse tribes, were pushed off their land and made to live on what we call reservations. Throughout our country's history, many people have been treated with hate and fear because of their skin color or their ethnic background—this is terribly wrong. Treating people in this way is a violation of their dignity as children of God."

Sister Bridget shook her head sadly and
turned to face the class. "Okay. Now let's
get back to the map. Who can name the
steps that brought you and your family
to this place, here, today? Can you trace
your family's geography?"

Everyone in the class chimed in. Lindsey's family had come from a village in northern China. Alejandro's grandfather had come from Madrid. Emmanuella's mom had come from Nigeria to finish college. Some people, including Sam and Sister Bridget herself, had families from Ireland.

As the discussion ended, Sister Bridget said, "You know, most of our families came to the U.S. from other countries and faced hate and mistreatment when they arrived. This was a very common experience. I'm sad to say that many people do not feel welcome in new places because they look or speak differently. We must change this."

The class was quiet. Sister Bridget looked thoughtful. "When we hurt one family with hateful words and actions, we hurt all families. Hate encourages hate. Love encourages love. Kids, I need to tell you, the vandalism that Ray's family experienced hurts all of us. We need to act with love."

Carmen spoke up. "Sister, we all have lots of things in common! We love our families. We like to play games. We celebrate special holidays. We eat foods that remind us of our grandparents or where our families came from. We like to visit places that mean a lot to us. We're all human beings. God made us all. Everyone belongs! If we focus on that, then maybe we can get rid of the hate."

Sam said, "Everyone belongs . . . we should go spray-paint that on garage doors."

Sister Bridget snapped her fingers. "No more graffiti, but that gives me an idea, Sam!" She went to the cupboard and pulled out art supplies. "I want you to make *Everyone Belongs* signs. We can plaster them all over the neighborhood. We'll act with love in the face of hate."

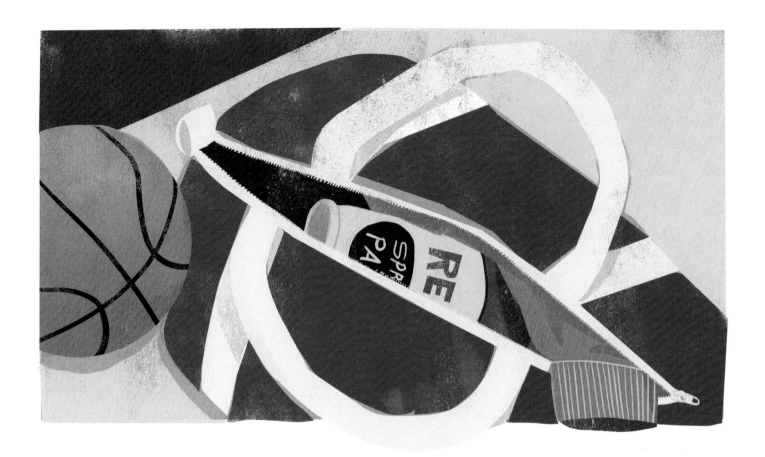

Ray didn't come to school for the rest of the week. On Friday afternoon, Sam's mom called Mrs. Ikanga. "How is Ray?" she asked.

"Ready to get out of the house," Mrs. Ikanga replied.

The boys decided to play basketball that afternoon. Sam hunted through his closet to find his sweatshirt before he remembered that the sweatshirt was in Carter's duffel bag. He found it in Carter's room. Sam was thinking about how good it would feel to get back to normal when he spotted the can.

Red spray paint.

Carter. *Carter!*

Sam felt a wave of anger and shame as he coasted on his bike down the hill to Ray's house. He rolled into the driveway, and Ray ran out to meet him.

"Am I glad to see you!" said Ray. "You know how my dad said I was a turtle? That's exactly what I've felt like all week. A little closed-up turtle. A turtle who's ready to come out of his shell." Ray laughed a bit.

Sam swallowed hard and tried to smile.

While the boys were shooting hoops, Sam thought about what Sister Bridget had said about acting with love. It would be easy to do nothing—to pretend that what he suspected his brother had done was no big deal. But he couldn't do that to Ray, and he couldn't do it to himself, either. He had to find the courage to speak up.

When Carter got home, Sam met him on the porch. "I know what you did."

Carter started to shove by. "You don't know anything."

"I know you scared and hurt my friend. I know you scared and hurt all of us," said Sam.

"Hurt us? I'm helping us," said Carter. "Dad's been out of work for months."

"What does that have to do with anything?" asked Sam angrily.

Carter folded his arms. "Don't you see? It's because of people like the Ikangas that Dad's having trouble. If outsiders get the jobs, they'll change everything. There won't be anything left for people like us."

Sam couldn't believe his ears. "People like us? Carter, the Ikangas *are* people like us. We're all human beings. This isn't like a sport with different teams." He shook his head. "The Ikangas aren't going to take anything away from us—and they add so much. If you don't make this right, I will."

The boys stood perfectly still, Sam staring Carter directly in the eye. *Come on, Carter. You can understand this. Love encourages love,* thought Sam.

After what seemed like a long time, Sam saw a slight slump in Carter's shoulders. Carter's eyes filled with tears.

Carter did understand—he knew he had done wrong. He had sinned against the Ikangas, his family, and his entire community.

Sam could see that Carter was now ready to take responsibility for what he had done. "Come on, Carter," said Sam, "I have an idea about how to make things right. I might be your little brother, but now I'm going to coach you."

On Saturday afternoon, friends from the parish and the soccer team joined the Ikangas for a community gathering followed by a house blessing.

Before the celebration began, Father Mateo held up his hand to get everyone's attention. "I want to thank you all for coming. I had a long visit with Carter this week, and he has something he wants to say."

Shifting nervously from one foot to the other, Carter apologized to the Ikangas and the community and asked their forgiveness. Everyone was quiet as he spoke. Then Carter turned to Dr. Ikanga and shook his steady hand. As they spoke, Carter felt something change in his heart.

Then Father Mateo invited everyone to pick up a paintbrush from a pile at his feet.
"We have a chance to show that everyone belongs," he said, gesturing to the signs
hanging from the porches and light poles. "Now let's paint this garage together."
Dr. Ikanga and Carter each rolled a stroke of sunny yellow paint onto the garage door,
covering the hateful words for good.

When everyone had finished painting, Father Mateo offered a house blessing. "Now let us pray.

Lord God, from whom all good things come, keep all who enter here in peace and make this a house of true hospitality. Let us welcome the stranger, give drink to those who are thirsty, and give food to those who are hungry. Make us peacemakers in your image. We ask this through Christ our Lord. Amen."

After making the Sign of the Cross, everyone cheered. Sam and Ray joined the hungry crowd in line for food. "I'm proud to be your friend, Ray, and I'm so glad we're here together," said Sam.

"Where everyone belongs," Ray said.